Mice and Beans

BY Pam Muñoz Ryan

ILLUSTRATED BY Joe Cepeda

SCHOLASTIC INC.

NEW YORK   TORONTO   LONDON   AUCKLAND   SYDNEY
MEXICO CITY   NEW DELHI   HONG KONG   BUENOS AIRES

Rosa María lived in a tiny house with a tiny yard. But she had a big heart, a big family, and more than anything, she loved to cook big meals for them.

In one week, her youngest grandchild, Little Catalina, would be seven years old, and the whole family would squeeze into her *casita* for the party.

Rosa María didn't mind because she believed what her mother had always said: "When there's room in the heart, there's room in the house, **except** for a mouse."

Sunday, Rosa María planned the menu: *enchiladas*, rice and beans (no dinner was complete without rice and beans!), birthday cake, lemonade, and a *piñata* filled with candy.

She ordered the birthday present – something Little Catalina had wanted for a long time.

Satisfied with the plans, she wiped down the table so she wouldn't get mice and took out a mousetrap just in case. She was sure she had set one the night before, but now she couldn't find it. Maybe she'd forgotten.

When it was set and ready to snap, she turned off the light and went to bed.

Monday, Rosa María did the laundry. She washed and ironed her largest tablecloth and the twenty-four napkins that matched. But when she finished, she only counted twenty-three.

"*No importa*," she said. "It doesn't matter. So what if someone has a napkin that doesn't match? The important thing is that we're all together."

After dinner she swept the floor and checked the mousetrap.

But it was missing.

Didn't I set one last night? she wondered.

She hurried to the cupboard to fetch another, and when it was set and ready to **snap**, she turned off the light and went to bed.

Tuesday, Rosa María walked to the market. She filled her big *bolsa* with *tortillas*, cheese, red sauce, white rice, pinto beans, and a bag of candy. She bought a *piñata* and on her way home she stopped at the *pastelería* to order the cake.

After dinner, she washed the dishes and checked the mousetrap.

But it had vanished.

"*¡Qué boba soy!* Silly me, I must have forgotten, again!"

She hurried to the cupboard to fetch another and when it was set and ready to snap, she turned off the light and went to bed.

𝒲𝑒𝒹𝓃𝑒𝓈𝒹𝒶𝓎, Rosa María prepared the *enchiladas*. She dipped the *tortillas* in red sauce, filled them with cheese, and rolled them into fat little bundles. She noticed the *piñata* was missing a few feathers.

"*No importa*," she said. "Those feathers won't make a difference to the children when the *piñata* is filled with candy."

After dinner she mopped up the sauce and checked the mousetrap.

But it was gone again!

"I am so busy that I'm forgetting to remember!" she cried.

She hurried to the cupboard to fetch another and when it was set and ready to snap, she turned off the light and went to bed.

Thursday, Rosa María simmered the beans. She searched

for her favorite wooden spoon, the one she always used to
cook *frijoles*, but she couldn't find it.

"*No importa*," she said. "The beans will taste just
as good if I use another spoon."

She added water all day long until the beans
were plump and soft. Then she scrubbed the
stove and checked the mousetrap.

But it was nowhere in sight!

"*¡Cielos!*" she said. "Heavens!
Where is my mind?"

She hurried to the cupboard to
fetch another and when it was set
and ready to **snap**, she turned
off the light and went to bed.

Friday, Rosa María picked up the cake and seven candles. But she hadn't been able to find her big *bolsa* before she left.

"*No importa*," she said. "I'll carry the cake in one hand and the candles in the other."

Tomorrow was the big day. Rosa María knew she mustn't forget anything, so she carefully went over the list one last time.

After dinner she wrapped the cake and checked the mousetrap. She couldn't believe her eyes.

No mousetrap!

"Thank goodness I've got plenty."

She hurried to the cupboard to fetch another and when it was set and ready to **snap**, she turned off the light and went to bed.

Saturday, Rosa María cooked the rice. As the workers assembled Little Catalina's present, she set the table and squeezed the juiciest lemons from her tree.

"Let's see," she said, feeling very proud. "*Enchiladas*, rice and beans (no dinner was complete without rice and beans!), birthday cake, and lemonade. I know I have forgotten something, but what? **The candles!**"

But she only counted six.

"*No importa*," she said. "I will arrange the six candles in the shape of a seven and Little Catalina will be just as happy. **Now**, everything is ready."

But
WAS
everything
ready
?

That afternoon Rosa María's family filled her tiny *casita*.
They ate the *enchiladas* and rice and beans. They drank
the fresh-squeezed lemonade. And they devoured the cake.

Little Catalina loved her present – a swing set! And after
every cousin had a turn, they chanted, "*¡La piñata! ¡La piñata!*"

They ran to the walnut tree and
threw a rope over a high
branch.

Whack! Whack! Little Catalina swung the *piñata* stick.

"Wait!" cried Rosa María as she remembered what she'd forgotten. But it was too late.

Crack! The *piñata* separated, and the children scrambled to collect the candy.

How could that be? Rosa María puzzled. I must have filled it without even realizing!

She laughed at her own forgetfulness as she hugged her granddaughter and said, "*Feliz cumpleaños*, my Little Catalina. Happy birthday."

After everyone had gone, Rosa María tidied her kitchen and thought contentedly about the *fiesta*. She pictured the happy look on Little Catalina's face when the candy spilled from the *piñata*. But Rosa María still couldn't remember when she had filled it.

"*No importa*," she said. "It was a wonderful day."

But as Rosa María swept out the cupboard, she discovered the telltale signs of mice!

"*¡Ratones!*" she cried. "Where are my mousetraps? I will set them all!"

She inched to the floor and when she did, something caught her eye.

She looked closer.

Maybe I **didn't** fill the *piñata*, she thought.

"Was it possible?" she asked, shaking her head.
"Could I have had help?"

Rosa María looked at the leftovers. Too much
for one person.

And what was it her mother had always said?
"When there's room in the heart, there's room
in the house . . . even for a mouse."

"¡Fíjate! Imagine that!" she said. "I
remembered the words wrong all these
years."

Besides, how many could there be?
Two? Four?

"No importa," she said. "It doesn't
matter if a few helpful mice live here,
too."

Then she turned off the light and
went to bed . . .

... and never set another mousetrap again.